THE EXTRAORDINARY FILES

Werewolf Eclipse

Paul Blum

RISING★STARS

'The Truth is inside us.
It is the only place where it can hide.'

nasen

NASEN House, 4/5 Amber Business Village, Amber Close,
Amington, Tamworth, Staffordshire B77 4RP

Rising Stars UK Ltd.
22 Grafton Street, London W1S 4EX
www.risingstars-uk.com

Text © Rising Stars UK Ltd.
The right of Paul Blum to be identified as the author of this work has
been asserted by him in accordance with the Copyright, Design and
Patents Act 1988.

Published 2007
Reprinted 2008

Cover design: Button plc
Illustrator: Enzo Troiano
Text design and typesetting: pentacorbig
Publisher: Gill Budgell
Project management and editorial: Lesley Densham
Editor: Maoliosa Kelly
Editorial consultant: Lorraine Petersen

British Library Cataloguing in Publication Data.
A CIP record for this book is available from the British Library.

ISBN: 978 1 84680 180 8

Printed by Craft Print International Limited, Singapore

CHAPTER ONE

Mexico City

Hundreds of people had come to see the eclipse.
As the shadow fell over the city, FBI agents looked
for a murderer. They knew he would be there.
Would they get him before he killed again?

It was just three minutes to the total eclipse. Three
minutes to when the sun passed behind the moon.
Three minutes to when the day would become dark
and silent. But the agents lost the race against time.
The murderer killed five people in a back street.
It was as if they had been attacked by a wild animal.
One girl was badly bitten but luckily she lived.

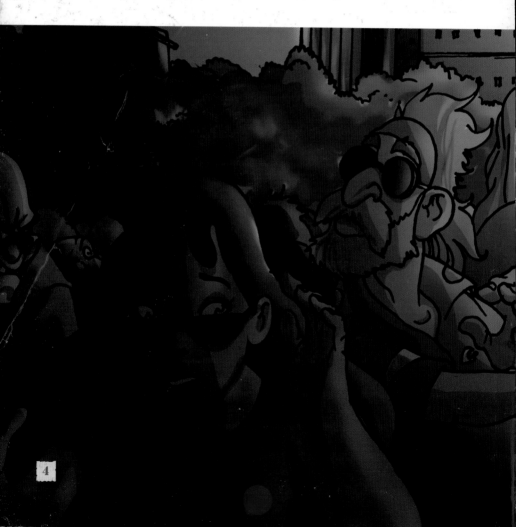

London Vauxhall. MI5 Headquarters.

Agent Parker and Agent Turnbull had been doing karate training for one hour.

"Parker, you are getting good at this," Turnbull said.

"Do you think so?" replied Parker.

"We will end with 50 sit-ups," she said.

"50, are you trying to kill me, Laura?" he moaned.

One hour later, they were having breakfast.

"You seem a lot more relaxed since you started working out," Turnbull said.

"I like it because we are spending a lot of time together," he replied.

"We are spending nearly 24 hours a day together. We may as well be married!" she laughed.

Robert Parker looked like he had been stung by a bee. He changed the subject quickly.

"So do you think I have the makings of a killer?" he asked.

"Not a chance, Parker. But if you want to see a terrible killer come and read about this new Mexico case."

They looked at the photos of the victims.

"The killings are always the same. They take place when there is a full eclipse of the sun, at the place of longest darkness. It was Mexico last year, Australia and Japan before that," she said.

"The victims were bitten and clawed and some dog hair was found on their skin," Parker said. "I think we could have a werewolf on our hands."

They were both silent.

"I was afraid you would say that," she said.

"And we have a total eclipse in Cornwall next week," he added. He checked the computer. "David Wood near St David will be the longest place of darkness. Three minutes and 25 seconds."

"What can we do?" she asked.

"Fly Angela Lopez over from Mexico. The girl who was badly bitten but lived. The story says that werewolves always come back to finish off their victims," he said.

"You want to use a young, frightened girl to trap the werewolf?" Turnbull said. "That's a terrible idea!"

"But we will be there when the murderer strikes. It's the only way to save other people's lives. Angela may be able to give us useful information," he said.

"It says here that she can't remember anything!" Turnbull read.

"Her memory may come back when the eclipse begins," he said. "The werewolf will be near then."

"I don't like it," Turnbull said, shivering.

"Nor do I, but it's our only chance."

CHAPTER TWO

They met Angela Lopez at the airport. They took her to London. She was happy to help them.

"I can't remember anything about the attack," she said.
"All I remember is waking up in hospital. Will that do?"

The agents nodded kindly and left her to rest.

Parker made plans. There was a lot to think about. Over two million people would be going to Cornwall to watch the eclipse. They had to stop the murderer from hiding in the crowd.

"We will trap him in David Wood. If he's a werewolf he will want to get near Angela. He will smell her blood," Parker said.

"You and your werewolves!" said Turnbull.

The next day, they went to St David. Angela tried to help Parker and Turnbull but she could not remember anything useful. Angela looked tired.

"Agent Turnbull, have you seen Angela? She is acting in a strange way."

"She seems ok to me."

"She is getting weaker. The werewolf must be nearby."

"Maybe she is just bored with you," Turnbull laughed.

"There are only 24 hours to go to the eclipse. Let's hope she remembers something quickly. We really need some help," he said.

It was the evening before the eclipse. The two agents were watching television with Angela. Suddenly she began to sweat.

"Angela, what's wrong?" shouted Turnbull.

"I feel shivers down my spine. It feels like claws in my back," she sobbed.

"Can you see him, Angela?" Parker asked.

She nodded.

"Can you draw him?"

She nodded again.

They put her on the sofa. They covered her with a blanket. She drew a picture onto some paper. Parker grabbed it.

"I'll be back in a second, Angela," he said.

Turnbull stayed with her and held her hand.

Parker ran into the other room. He fed the paper into his laptop computer.

"It can't be true. It can't be true," he muttered to himself. "Turnbull, come and look at this."

Turnbull ran in. "What is it?"

"Look carefully," he said, pointing at the screen.

"It looks like a picture of a dog to me," she said.

"You mean a werewolf," he said.

"I *had* worked that out, Parker."

"But look at its face," he said.

"I don't get you."

"Look carefully."

"Alright, alright, give me a chance," she replied.

"What do you see?"

"I told you – a shaggy dog."

He clicked a button on his computer. "Now what do you see?"

"Oh no, no," she moaned. "It can't be."

"It's Angela Lopez," he whispered.

Just then, they heard a window smashing. They ran into the sitting room. Angela had jumped out into the night. There were some dog hairs on the carpet.

CHAPTER THREE

Parker got on the phone to the police.

"Security alert. Murder suspect is Angela Lopez.
She is dressed in a red shirt and brown trousers when
last seen. She will look very strange. She has hair all
over her face and very long teeth. Do not go near her.
She is very dangerous!"

Angela ran through David Wood. She was howling like a wolf. Her arms and legs were getting longer. Her face was growing hair. She was becoming a werewolf!

Parker was shocked. "I should have guessed. Anyone
who is bitten by a werewolf, and lives, becomes
a werewolf."

"It wasn't your fault," Turnbull said.

Parker and Turnbull pushed through the crowds of people.

Parker looked at his watch and then at the sky.

"The sun is moving behind the moon. It's beginning," he whispered. Then Parker's mobile rang.

"Angela Lopez has been seen in David Wood!" he shouted. "We've got her. The wood is blocked off."

They ran towards the wood. When they got there, the eclipse was starting. The sky was getting darker. The flowers had closed up. The birds had stopped singing.

"Let us through!" Turnbull shouted.

"Nobody is allowed through," said the policeman.

"So where is she going?" screamed Parker.
He pointed to a woman with a child in a pram.

"Oh, I said she could use the toilet. The kid needs a nappy change."

Turnbull and Parker pushed past him and ran towards the toilet. It was completely dark now.

"Get out of there!" screamed Turnbull.

They dragged the woman and child away from the toilets. The child started to cry.

Suddenly they heard a wolf's howl. A big animal jumped out at them. Turnbull kicked it in the back. The werewolf turned on her. It snapped at her face.

One shot rang out and the werewolf fell down.
There was the sound of screaming and panic.
The police ran towards them with torches. Just then,
the sun passed from behind the moon. Daylight
returned. The eclipse was over.

The werewolf was dead. They stood watching it as it slowly turned back into Angela Lopez. Parker sobbed when he saw her. Turnbull comforted him. The police took the mother and child away.

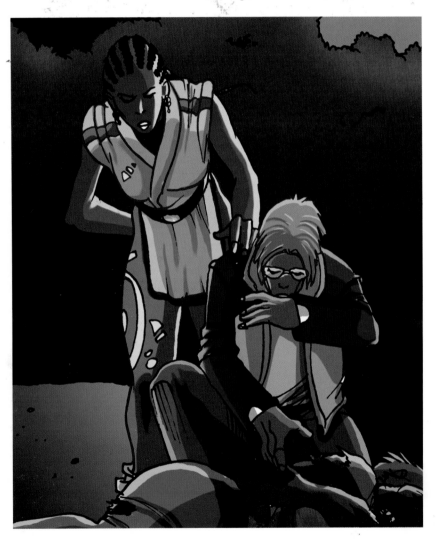

CHAPTER FOUR

Two days later, Turnbull and Parker were back in their office.

"So how are the mother and child?" asked Parker.

"The mother is fine. The girl has a cut on her arm," said Turnbull.

"A cut?" Parker asked nervously.

"It could be a bite. It could be a scratch. They are not going to take any chances," Turnbull said.

"What does that mean exactly?" he said.

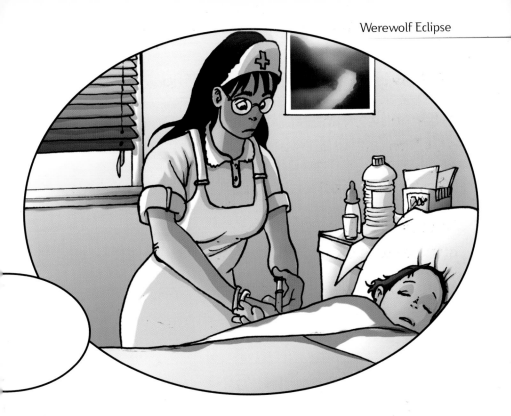

"It means they are going to kill the child," she said in a whisper.

"Because of what it might become? That's terrible!" he shouted.

"The commander said it would be top secret. There will be an accident. The child's mother will never know."

"Oh, that makes it alright then. When will they do it?" Parker demanded.

"Tomorrow night," Turnbull whispered.

Parker knew what he had to do. He went to the hospital.

He got past the police guards using his ID. He got the little girl. He put her in a blanket and drove her home.

"What's my darling little Rosie doing here? The hospital told me that they still had tests to do," said her mother.

Parker spoke in a low voice. He had covered his face with a scarf. "Take her. Don't ask any questions. You must go away from here and never come back."

"But ..." the mother replied.

"No 'buts'! Rosie's life is in danger. Just take her away. Don't ask me who I am. Just think of me as her fairy godmother."

He handed the child over quickly and disappeared.

When he got back, Turnbull was waiting for him. "I know what you have done," she said.

"You do?" he replied.

"I don't blame you. Every human being has the right to life."

Parker nodded. "I hope I did the right thing. I could not let them kill a child. She looked so sweet. If the commander finds out what I did, I am finished!"

"You were with me all day and you never went out of my sight," Turnbull said.

Rosie had her second birthday a few months later. Agent Parker and Turnbull were not there to see her on this happy day. She was in the garden. The family dog came up to her and wagged its tail. It sniffed her and then it howled. The hair on its back stood up and it ran out of the garden.

GLOSSARY OF TERMS

eclipse the period of time when the Sun's light and heat is obscured by the Moon passing in front of it.

fairy godmother someone who has a person's best interests at heart

FBI Federal Bureau of Investigation

karate a Japanese martial art which uses hands and feet as weapons

murder suspect the person thought to be the killer

not going to take any chances not to leave anything to risk

security alert a warning to police to be on their guard

to change the subject to introduce a new topic of conversation

top secret highly confidential

victim person injured or killed

werewolf a human being who has turned into a wolf

QUIZ

1　What happened in Mexico city?

2　Why does Parker think the murderer is a werewolf?

3　How long is the eclipse at St David Wood in Cornwall?

4　Why does Angela Lopez turn into a werewolf?

5　Who does the werewolf attack?

6　What did the commander say was top secret?

7　Who did Parker give the child to?

8　Why did Rosie's dog run out of the garden?

9　How many werewolves are there in the story?

ABOUT THE AUTHOR

Paul Blum has taught for over 20 years in London inner-city schools.

I wrote The Extraordinary Files for my pupils so they've been tested by some fierce critics (you!). That's why I know you'll enjoy reading them.

I've made the stories edgy in terms of character and content and I've written them using the kind of fast-paced dialogue you'll recognise from television soaps. I hope you'll find The Extraordinary Files an interesting and easy-to-read collection of stories.

ANSWERS TO QUIZ

1 There was an eclipse, five people were murdered and one girl was badly bitten but lived

2 The victims were bitten and clawed and there were dog hairs on their skin

3 Three minutes and 25 seconds

4 It is the time of an eclipse and she was bitten by a werewolf in Mexico but lived

5 It attacks a mother and child

6 They plan to kill the child to stop her growing up into a werewolf

7 Parker gave the child to her mother

8 It ran out of the garden because it sensed that Rosie was a werewolf

9 Four: one in Australia, one in Japan, Angela Lopez in Mexico, and Rosie in Cornwall